The Itsy Bitsy Spider

Illustrated by
Joe & Terri Chicko

Sadlier-Oxford
A Division of William H. Sadlier, Inc.
New York, NY 10005-1002

The itsy bitsy spider

climbed up the water spout.

Down came the rain

and washed the spider out.

Out came the sun
and dried up all the rain.

And the itsy bitsy spider
climbed up the spout again.